FUNNYBONES

Janet & Allan Ahlberg

PUFFIN BOOKS

This is how the story begins.
On a dark dark hill
there was a dark dark town.
In the dark dark town
there was a dark dark street.
In the dark dark street
there was a dark dark house.
In the dark dark house
there was a dark dark staircase.
Down the dark dark staircase
there was a dark dark cellar.
And in the dark dark cellar ...

... some skeletons lived.

There was a big skeleton,
a little skeleton and a dog skeleton.

One night the big skeleton
sat up in bed.
He scratched his skull.
"What shall we do tonight?" he said.
"Let's take the dog for a walk,"
said the little skeleton.
"And frighten somebody!"
"Good idea!" the big skeleton said.

So the big skeleton,
the little skeleton
and the dog skeleton
left the dark dark cellar,
climbed the dark dark staircase
and stepped out into the dark dark street.

They walked past the houses
and the shops.
They walked past the zoo
and the police station.
They went into the park.

The big skeleton scratched his skull.
"What shall we do now?" he said.
"Let's play on the swings,"
said the little skeleton.
"And throw a stick for the dog –
and frighten somebody!"
"Good idea!" the big skeleton said.

WHAT SHALL WE DO NOW?

So the big skeleton,
the little skeleton and the dog skeleton
walked round the dark dark pond,
past the dark dark tennis courts
and up to the dark dark swings.

LET'S PLAY ON THE SWINGS

The big skeleton and the little skeleton
played on the swings.
They threw a stick for the dog.

Suddenly something happened.
The dog skeleton chased the stick,
tripped over a park bench,
bumped into a tree –

and ended up as a little pile of bones.

"Look at that!" the big skeleton said.
"He's all come to pieces.
What shall we do now?"
"Let's put him together again,"
the little skeleton said.
So the big skeleton
and the little skeleton
put the dog skeleton together again.
They sang a song while they did it.

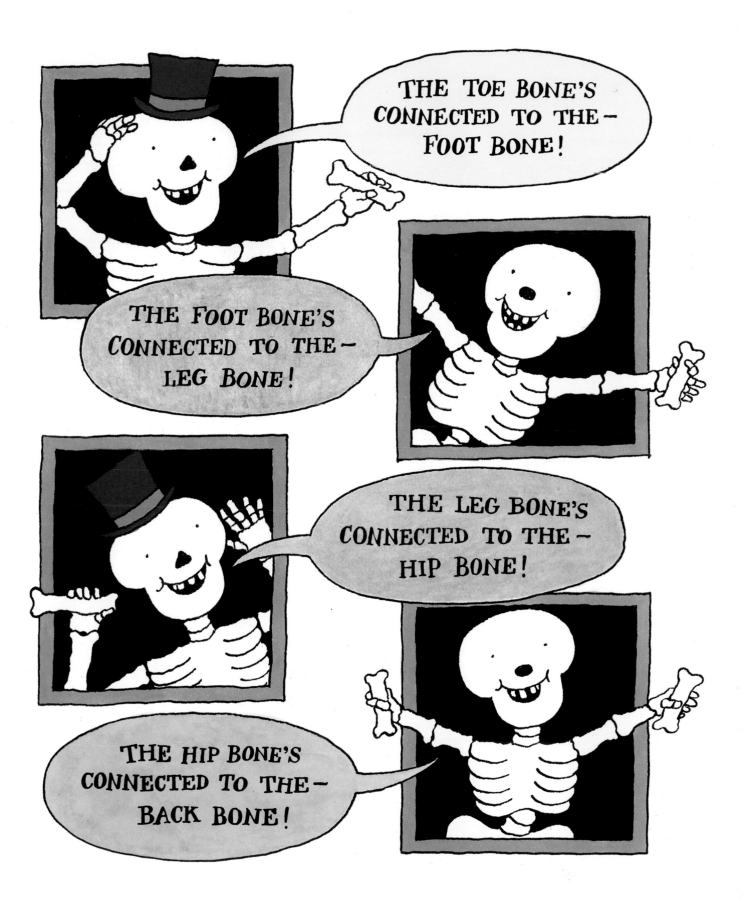

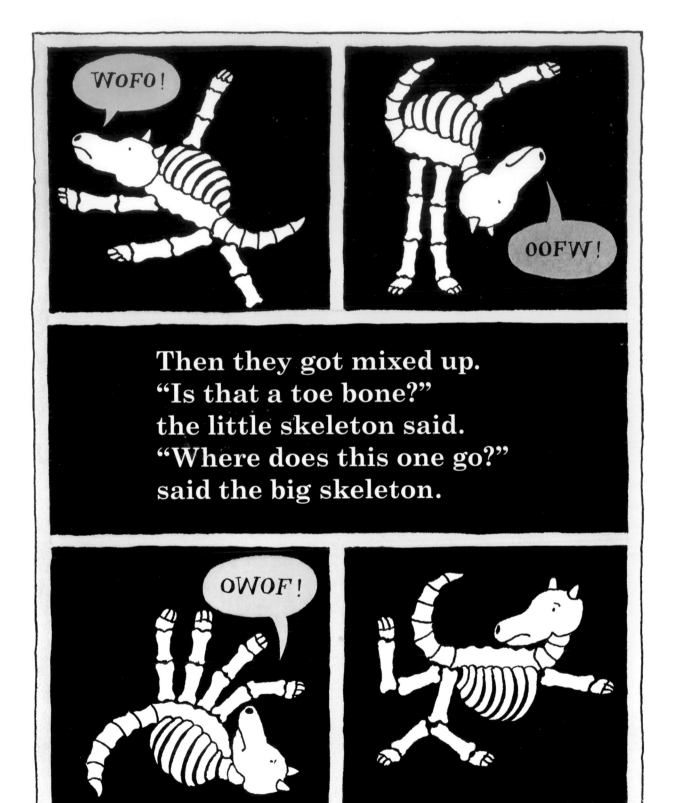

Then they got mixed up.
"Is that a toe bone?"
the little skeleton said.
"Where does this one go?"
said the big skeleton.

When they had finished, the big
skeleton said,
"That dog looks a bit funny to me."
"So he does," said the little skeleton.
"We've got his tail on the wrong end –
and his head!"
"Foow!" said the dog skeleton.

At last the dog was properly
put back together again.
The big skeleton and the little skeleton
sang another song.

THESE BONES, THESE BONES CAN
BARK AGAIN!
CAN RUN AROUND IN THE
PARK AGAIN!
CAN FRIGHTEN PEOPLE IN THE
DARK AGAIN!

The big skeleton scratched his skull.
"That reminds me," he said.
"We forgot to frighten somebody!"
"Let's do it on the way home, then,"
said the little skeleton.
"Good idea!" the big skeleton said.

So the big skeleton,
the little skeleton and the dog skeleton
left the dark dark swings,
went out into the dark dark town –
and tried to frighten somebody.

The trouble was, there wasn't anybody.
Everybody was in bed.
Even the policemen in the police
station were in bed.
Even the animals in the zoo!
Of course, the *skeleton* animals
were awake.

"Let's have a ride on the elephant
skeleton," the little skeleton said.
"Let's have a word with the parrot
skeleton."
The big skeleton scratched his skull.
"Let's ... keep out of the way
of the crocodile skeleton," he said.

When they were back in the street, and when they still could not find anybody to frighten, the big skeleton said, "What shall we do now?"

The little skeleton scratched *his* skull.
"Let's frighten each other!" he said.
"That's better than nothing!"
"Good idea!" the big skeleton said.

So after that the big skeleton
frightened the little skeleton,
the little skeleton
frightened the big skeleton,
the big skeleton and the little skeleton
frightened the dog skeleton,
and the dog skeleton frightened them.

They hid round corners
and frightened each other.
They climbed up lamp posts
and frightened each other.
They jumped out of dustbins
and frightened each other –

And that is how the story ends.
On a dark dark hill
there was a dark dark town.
In the dark dark town
there was a dark dark street.
In the dark dark street
there was a dark dark house.
In the dark dark house
there was a dark dark staircase.
Down the dark dark staircase
there was a dark dark cellar.
In the dark dark cellar
some skeletons lived.

They still do.

THE END

PUFFIN BOOKS

Published by the Penguin Group
Penguin Books Ltd, 80 Strand, London WC2R 0RL, England
Penguin Group (USA), Inc., 375 Hudson Street, New York, New York 10014, USA
Penguin Books Australia Ltd, 250 Camberwell Road, Camberwell, Victoria 3124, Australia
Penguin Books Canada Ltd, 10 Alcorn Avenue, Toronto, Ontario, Canada M4V 3B2
Penguin Books India (P) Ltd, 11 Community Centre, Panchsheel Park, New Delhi – 110 017, India
Penguin Group (NZ), cnr Airborne and Rosedale Roads, Albany, Auckland 1310, New Zealand
Penguin Books (South Africa) (Pty) Ltd, 24 Sturdee Avenue, Rosebank 2196, South Africa

Penguin Books Ltd, Registered Offices: 80 Strand, London WC2R 0RL, England

www.penguin.com

First published by William Heinemann Ltd 1980
Published in Puffin Books 1999
13 15 17 19 20 18 16 14

Text and illustrations copyright © Janet & Allan Ahlberg, 1980
All rights reserved

Set in Century Schoolbook Monotype Bold 20/25pt

Printed and bound in China by South China Printing Co.

British Library Cataloguing in Publication Data
A CIP catalogue record for this book is available from the British Library

ISBN 0–140–56581–7